Monsters Not Allowed!

Tracey Hammett & Jan McCafferty

Monsters not Allowed. Published in Great Britain 2020 by Graffeg Limited.

Written by Tracey Hammett copyright © 2010. Illustrated by Jan McCafferty copyright © 2010. Produced by Graffeg Limited copyright © 2020. First published in 2010 by Scholastic Children's Books.

Graffeg Limited, 15 Neptune Court, Vanguard Way, Cardiff CF24 5PJ. Wales UK. Tel: sales +44(0)1554 824000 www.graffeg.com

Tracey Hammett and Jan McCafferty are hereby identified as the authors of this work in accordance with section 77 of the Copyrights, Designs and Patents Act 1988. A CIP Catalogue record for this book is available from the British Library.

ISBN 9781913134341

1 2 3 4 5 6 7 8 9

To one very precious Ruby,
A huddle of heart-warming Hammetts
And a cluster of lovely friends (big and small)
Who have helped me - one and all ~ TH

With all my love to Lara Pippa who appears in this book!
Also to Kit, kisses ~ JM

Monsters
Not Allowed!

Written by
Tracey Hammett

Illustrated by
Jan McCafferty

GRAFFEG

A **monster** came to school one day.

FIDGET
SCHOOL

It tiptoed through the gate . . .

It slunk into the classroom
Grunting, "Sorry, Monster late!"

"What's your name?" Miss Harbord asked.
It said, **"Monster forgot,"**

And while she called the register
It scratched its you-know-what.

It stomped into assembly
And did a funny walk,

While Mr Jedd the Deputy Head
Was giving a serious talk.

And then in silent reading,
While the class behaved so well,

It let out lots of silly sounds
And made a stinky smell!

It yammered, yipped and yodelled,

It warbled, whooped and whined,

Miss Harbord kept it in at play,
But the monster didn't mind.

We gave it our packed lunches
And it snaffled up the lot,

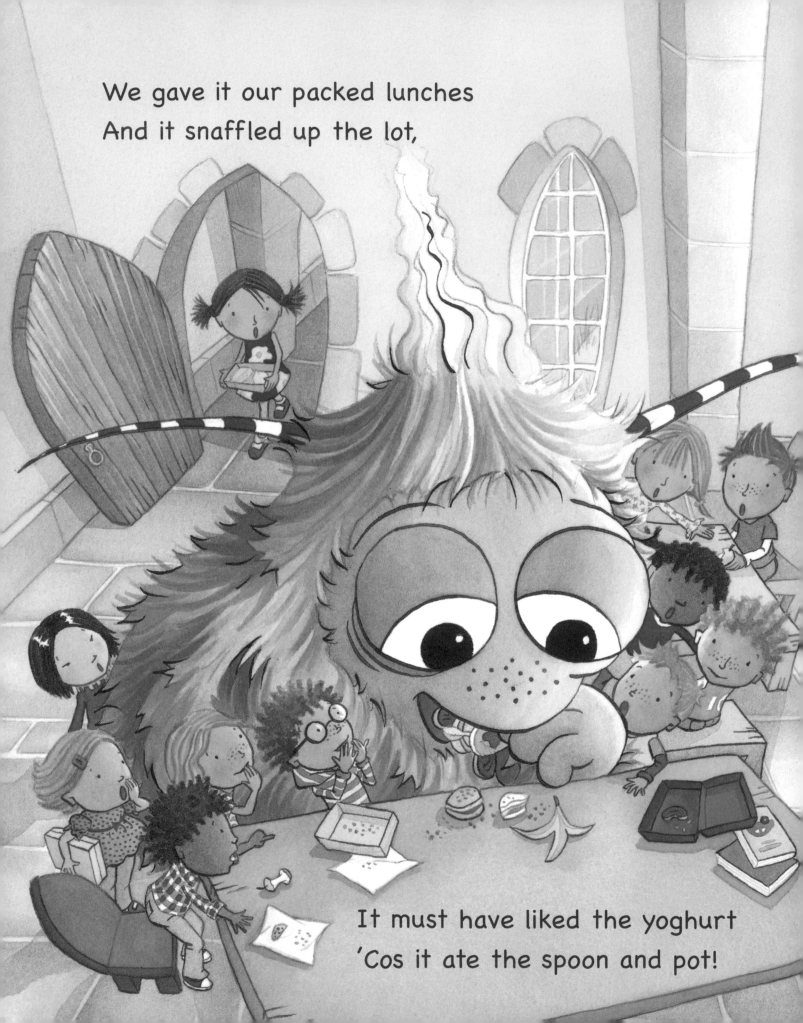

It must have liked the yoghurt
'Cos it ate the spoon and pot!

"That's not the way to eat your lunch!
Now sit up nicely, please,"
Said Mr Jedd the Deputy Head
As the monster scratched its fleas.

We had a game of football
And the monster scored a goal,

Then in PE we taught it how
To do a forward roll.

Each morning as we sat in class,
Our monster would appear,

And when we saw its funny face,
We'd all begin to cheer!

Then Mr Jedd the Deputy Head
Got very cross one day,

So he made a great big sign that said:

The monster sobbed a monster sob
And wandered down the street,

It hung its funny monster head
And dragged its monster feet.

And all at once the school went quiet —
You couldn't hear a sound.
Nobody sang, or skipped, or ran,
Or chased the leaves around.

The children wouldn't do their work,
Or play a football game,

We didn't even want our lunch —
It didn't taste the same.

"I take it back!" said Mr Jedd.
He shed a tiny tear,

"Let's find the monster right away,
And bring it straight back here!"

We all worked hard in school that day
And everyone stayed late,

We painted monster posters
And we hung them on the gate . . .

Have you seen this monster
Skulking down the street?
It has eyes as big as frisbees
And funny, bumpy feet.

Miss Harbord found the monster,
It didn't take her long . . .

She spied it in the supermarket,
Singing silly songs!

And when we brought it back to school,
It grunted, **"Monster stay!"**

So now it's joined our class for good,
And it comes in every day.

"I'm glad the monster came to school —
It's everybody's friend,"
Said Mr Jedd the Deputy Head,
Who liked it in the end.

Fidget School
END OF YEAR REPORT
Name: Monster

Mr & Mrs Monster
Googly Lane, Monsterville

Spelling:	Monstrous... but top marks for trying
Maths:	Incredible counting
P.E.:	Fantastic football skills and fabulous forward rolls
Music:	Ear splitting yodelling and splendid yammers and yips
Art:	Superb paint splattering
Effort:	Outstanding. Monster is always smiley and kind to everyone.

WELL DONE

for . . .

✓ Doing all your homework

✓ Only eating your own lunch

✓ Not breaking any furniture

✓ Being a wonderful friend

✓ Just being you!

✓ Working really hard

The End